Back on the Beam

Eric Stevens

illustrated by Tuesday Mourning

Raintree

www.raintreepublishers.co.uk
Visit our website to find out
more information about
Raintree books.

To order:
☎ Phone 0845 6044371
📄 Fax +44 (0) 1865 312263
🖳 Email myorders@capstonepub.co.uk

Customers from outside the UK please telephone +44 1865 312262

Raintree is an imprint of Capstone Global Library Limited, a company incorporated in
England and Wales having its registered office at 7 Pilgrim Street, London, EC4V 6LB –
Registered company number: 6695582

"Raintree" is a registered trademark of Pearson Education Limited, under licence to
Capstone Global Library Limited

Text © Stone Arch Books 2009
First published by Stone Arch Books in 2009
First published in hardback and paperback in the United Kingdom by
Capstone Global Library in 2010
The moral rights of the proprietor have been asserted.

Edited in the United Kingdom by Diyan Leake
Original illustrations © Stone Arch Books 2009
Illustrated by Tuesday Mourning
Originated by Capstone Global Library Ltd
Printed in China by Leo Paper Products Ltd

ISBN 978 1 4062 1385 0 (hardback)
14 13 12 11 10
10 9 8 7 6 5 4 3 2 1

ISBN 978 1 4062 1406 2 (paperback)
14 13 12 11 10
10 9 8 7 6 5 4 3 2 1

British Library Cataloguing in Publication Data
Stevens, Eric – Back on the beam
A full catalogue record for this book is available from the British Library.

Acknowledgements
We would like to thank the following for permission to reproduce photographs: Capstone
Press/Karon Dubke cover (background), p. 1 (background)

Every effort has been made to contact copyright holders of material reproduced in
this book. Any omissions will be rectified in subsequent printings if notice is given to
the publisher.

Contents

Chapter 1 Homework 5

Chapter 2 Trials 11

Chapter 3 First Warning 17

Chapter 4 Doomed. 25

Chapter 5 Second Warning 31

Chapter 6 Practice 39

Chapter 7 Nerves. 43

Chapter 8 The Competition 50

Chapter 9 Fun 58

About the author and illustrator. 64
Glossary 65
Female gymnastic events. 66
Gymnastics words you should know. 67
Discussion questions 68
Writing prompts 69
Other books in the series 70
Find out more. 72

CHAPTER 1

Homework

"This is boring," Nadia muttered to herself.

She sat on her bed, tapping her pencil on the notebook in her lap. Her maths textbook lay open on the pillow next to her.

It was the first maths homework of the school year, but she just couldn't do it. Her eyes were on the problems in the book, but her mind was miles away.

She glanced across the room. In the corner, in a cardboard box, was a plaster cast. It had been cut right down the middle. That's how the doctor had got it off Nadia's foot.

Signatures in purple, green, and pink felt-tip covered the cast. Every member of Nadia's gymnastics team had signed it. Well, every member except Claire Birch.

Nadia remembered when she got that cast. In fact, it seemed like it was all she could think about.

The last gymnastics competition the year before was the county finals. Nadia was on the Riverside School team, the Ravens. Nadia was one of the best on the balance beam. Her team had been counting on her and Claire Birch to help them win the finals.

Nadia stared at the first maths problem, but the line through the fractions reminded her of the beam. It also reminded her of her second attempt in the event at the county finals.

Nadia thought back to that day. Claire had already had two turns, and she scored an 8.9. It was a very good score, but not good enough to win the event for the Ravens.

That meant Nadia would have to do even better. She needed to score a 9.2. On her first attempt, she'd scored an 8.8.

Nadia chewed her pencil as she thought about that day. She remembered starting her routine. In the beginning, it had been perfect. She had practised it about a million times, after all.

But towards the end, she had made a little mistake. She wobbled a tiny bit on the beam.

"Nobody's perfect," she'd told herself. But her heart started pounding, and she was worried she wouldn't be good enough to win the event for her team.

Her nerves had bothered her all day. By the time she dismounted, she was so nervous that she messed up the landing. Her ankle twisted, and she landed in a lump on the mat. Suddenly she was in pain.

Nadia had screamed. Her best friends, Hannah and Alya, had run over to her from the sidelines.

Soon her mother was at her side too. Then Nadia was limping to the car and being driven to the hospital.

Before Nadia's mum drove away, though, Claire Birch had walked up to the car. "You made us lose, Nadia!" Claire had shouted at her. "Well done!"

For the rest of the summer, Nadia had been in that stupid cast. She was stuck at home while her friends took gymnastics classes. Alya had even gone off for two weeks to gymnastics camp. Nadia was jealous all summer.

Now that the cast was finally off, she thought she'd be glad. But instead, with gymnastics trials only one day away, she was nervous, not glad.

She hadn't been on the beam all summer. She had no idea how she'd be able to compete with all those girls at the trials the next day.

"There's no way I'll make the team," Nadia said to herself. She picked up her pencil and started on the first maths problem. "I might as well do my maths homework," she sighed.

CHAPTER 2

Trials

"Are you ready, Nadia?" Alya said as Nadia walked into the gym the next day after school.

Hannah added, "How's your ankle?"

Nadia shrugged. "It's a little sore, I guess," she said. "I'm just so out of shape."

Alya punched her lightly on the arm. "Come on," she joked. "It's like riding a bike. It comes right back in no time."

Hannah laughed. "Yeah," she added. "It's like falling off a log. Easy!"

Just then, Claire walked by. "Falling off a log, Hannah?" she asked. "If it's anything like falling off a balance beam, then I'm sure that Nadia will be great at it!"

Claire walked away, laughing. Nadia felt tears spring into her eyes.

"Don't let her get to you, Nadia," Alya said. "She's just feeling bad because she couldn't win the finals for us either."

"Exactly," Hannah agreed. "You've always been better on the beam, Nadia. She's your biggest competition at trials, and you'll beat her, definitely!"

"If you say so," Nadia said. She was still nervous about how out of shape she was.

All the girls from last year's team said hello and talked about their summers for a few minutes. Then the PE techer, Miss Wilkins, walked in and blew her whistle.

"All right, ladies," Miss Wilkins said. "Let's get started. Remember, keep it simple today. Save the dangerous stuff for the big time, okay?"

"Okay, Miss," the girls replied. A lot of them had been on the team before, Nadia noticed. There were a few girls she'd never seen before, though.

The girls all lined up. Miss Wilkins looked them over. "You all know how this works," she said. "The best five girls in each event will be on the team. If one girl is in the top five in more than one event, she will compete in both events. Got it?"

"Yes, Miss," the girls replied.

Miss Wilkins blew her whistle. Then the trials began.

Nadia went straight to the balance beam. "I better get through my beam routine before my ankle starts hurting," she said to Hannah.

"You're up, Nadia," Miss Wilkins said. "I'm glad to see your cast is off."

Nadia mounted into a split and started one of the routines she had practised last year. It wasn't a very hard routine, but one aerial tripped her up a little. Nadia wobbled as she landed and had to step off the beam so that she wouldn't fall. She heard Claire laughing at her.

"That's okay, Nadia," Alya called out. "Finish it!"

Nadia sighed and jumped back on to the beam. She finished the routine pretty well, and only took one extra step on the dismount.

Hannah smiled when Nadia was done. "You were great, Nadia," Hannah said.

Nadia shook her head. "I practically fell off," she said. "Claire was totally right. I'll never make the team this year."

CHAPTER 3

First Warning

The next morning, Nadia overslept. It was only by a few minutes, but she had to run the whole way to school. She wanted to get there early.

Miss Wilkins would be posting the names of the girls who had made the team. Hannah and Alya had promised to wait for Nadia in front of the school.

"I picked the worst day to oversleep," Nadia muttered to herself as she ran.

Finally, she went around the corner at Riverside Avenue and the school was in sight. Hannah and Alya waved as Nadia ran up to the school's front door.

"Finally!" Alya said.

"I can't believe you're late today. It's team-posting day!" Hannah cried, throwing her arms up. "Come on, let's get to Miss Wilkins' office."

Nadia nodded. "Let's go," she said. The three of them jogged past all the other students, who were looking through lockers and gathering books.

"First lesson starts in, like, two minutes," Hannah called out. "Hurry!"

By the time they reached Miss Wilkins' office, most of the other girls were already crowded around the list.

Hannah was the tallest of the three friends, so she peered over the heads of the other girls looking at the list.

"Yes!" Hannah cried out. "I'm on vault and bars!"

"Nice!" Alya said. "What about us?"

"Alya," Hannah said, "you're on floor."

"Great!" Alya shouted. She pumped her fist.

"And, Nadia," Hannah went on, "you made beam!"

"What?" a voice suddenly yelled. "Nadia fell and made the team anyway?" Nadia turned to see who had spoken. It was Claire, of course.

"Oh, be quiet, Claire," Alya said. She turned and faced Claire.

"No!" Claire replied. "I don't want a girl who can't even finish her routines on my beam team!"

"Your team?" Alya shouted back. She got right in Claire's face.

Miss Wilkins came out of her office. "What's going on here?" she shouted. Her face was red.

"Miss Wilkins," Claire said at once, stepping up to the coach, "how could you put Nadia on the beam team? Her performance at trials was horrible!"

Nadia shrank back. She wished she could just disappear into the walls.

"It was not horrible," Hannah said. "She just made one teeny tiny mistake."

"Ha!" Claire replied. "She fell off the beam!"

"That's enough, girls," Miss Wilkins said. She stepped between Hannah and Claire to separate them. "Everyone get to your lessons," Miss Wilkins said.

"Yes, Miss," they all replied. The girls started to break off and head towards their lessons.

"Nadia," the teacher added. "Wait a minute, okay?"

Hannah and Alya looked at Nadia. She waved them off. "I'll catch up," she said quietly.

As her friends walked off, Nadia turned to Miss Wilkins. "What is it, Miss?" she said.

"Nadia," the teacher replied, "I wanted to talk to you about your performance at the trials."

"I'm a little out of shape," Nadia explained. "I just got the cast off last week, so I haven't had any time to practise."

Miss Wilkins nodded. "I know," she said. "I'm giving you another chance because you were injured, but you'll need to work extra hard now."

"I know," Nadia said, nodding.

"I mean it," the teacher added. She put a hand on Nadia's shoulder and said, "If you don't show some quick improvement, I'm going to have to give your space on the beam team to someone else."

"What?" Nadia said, shocked.

"I'm sorry, Nadia," Miss Wilkins said. She started to head back into her office and added, "There are a lot of girls who'd like your space. We have to be fair, you know."

The office door closed with a thud. Nadia stood there, staring at it.

"I can't believe this," she muttered to herself. "I'm going to get kicked off the gymnastics team!"

Just then, the bell rang.

"Great," she said. "Now I'm late for my lesson."

Nadia turned and ran down the hall towards her first lesson.

CHAPTER 4

Doomed

It was burger day in the canteen. That meant dry, flat burgers with plastic cheese, and oily potato puffs. Nadia loved potato puffs. The dinner lady always gave her a few extra puffs.

Nadia grabbed a carton of milk and put it on her tray. Then she left the queue and looked for her friends. She spotted them sitting at a table in the corner by the windows.

Nadia plopped her tray down beside Hannah and Alya. "Hi, guys," she said.

"Hey, Nadia," Alya replied. "How's it going?"

Nadia was barely listening. She looked like her mind was miles away as she poked at her potato puffs. "This stinks," she said.

"Oh come on, Nadia," Alya replied. "You love potato puffs!"

"Yum," Hannah said, picking a puff off Nadia's tray. "Who doesn't love these things?" She pretended to eat the puff, then suddenly laughed and tossed it at Alya.

Alya shrieked and moved to one side. "Stop it!" she cried, laughing.

"The food isn't the problem, silly," Nadia said, rolling her eyes. "I'm going to get dropped from the team!"

"You are not," Hannah said. "Don't worry about what Miss Wilkins said. You'll be fine in no time."

"Yeah," Alya agreed. "It's not like you have to win a gold medal in the Olympics. You just have to be in the top five on the beam. That'll be easy for you."

"Exactly," Hannah said. "You're a natural."

Nadia shook her head. "I don't know," she said. "My ankle was kind of sore at trials. I think that's why I fell!"

Alya took one last bite of her burger. "I'm done," she announced. "Want to go outside for the rest of lunch? It's nice out."

Nadia sighed. "Sure," she said.

"Cheer up!" Hannah said. "The fresh air will do you good!"

The girls got up and carried their trays over to the tray rack. Suddenly, something bumped Nadia. Her tray dropped to the tile floor with a loud crash. Tomato ketchup and dirty plates flew everywhere. A splatter of milk landed on her trainers.

The whole canteen turned to look. Nadia felt her face getting hot.

"Oops," someone said behind Nadia. It was Claire Birch. "Seems like I lightly bumped into you."

"That was mean, Claire," Alya said. She stepped up to Claire and stared her down.

"Whatever. It was an accident," Claire replied, turning away from Alya. "It's not my fault your friend Nadia has zero balance."

Claire quickly spun towards Nadia. "You better work on your balance," she said. She jabbed her finger towards Nadia's face and added, "It's called a balance beam, you know. Not a falling beam." With that, Claire walked off, tossing her hair.

"Want me to knock her into the dustbin?" Alya said, glaring after Claire.

"No," Nadia replied sadly. Her shoulders sagged. "I think she's right. My balance is awful, and I'm doomed."

CHAPTER 5

Second Warning

The gymnastics team's first official practice was that day after school. The rest of the day dragged on and on for Nadia. She was excited to start practising, but nervous, too. When the bell rang, Nadia met Alya and Hannah in the locker room.

"Ugh, I hate the new team leotards," Alya said, standing in front of the mirror in her leotard. "Why can't we just wear last year's?"

Hannah shrugged. "The whole school council voted to change the school colours to orange and green, remember?" she said. "I don't know about you, but I kind of like them."

"What do you think, Nadia?" Alya asked. "Do you like the new colours?"

Nadia got up and went to the mirror. "Who cares?" she said. "I can't think about leotard colours right now. I'm too nervous."

"Well, I hate them," Alya said. "Though I must say, I do look good in every colour."

Hannah rolled her eyes. "Don't be nervous," she said, turning to Nadia. "I'm sure the wobble in trials won't happen again."

"Wobble?" Nadia replied. "You mean fall!"

"Fall, wobble," Hannah said. "Same thing. Just don't worry about it!"

"Yeah," Alya agreed. "If you're going to worry, worry about how silly we look in orange and green!"

A sharp whistle came from the gym. The girls looked at each other.

"We better get out there," Hannah said. "Sounds like practice is ready to start."

The three friends walked out of the locker room and into the gym. After stretching and warm-ups, Nadia joined the other four beam girls.

"Hello," Claire said to the group. "I'm the captain of the beam team this year. My name is Claire Birch."

The beam team girls looked at each other. Nadia frowned.

"Since when does the beam team have its own captain?" asked June. Nadia knew her from last year's team.

"Since I said so," Claire replied. "Now, first on the beam today will be Nadia. Everyone else practise your routines on the mat or the low beam. I'm going to watch Nadia and tell her everything she's doing wrong."

Nadia sighed deeply and walked up to the beam. As she mounted, her ankle started to hurt a little. She tried to ignore it.

Straight away, though, she was doing even worse than she had at trials. She could feel Claire watching her. Her ankle began to burn as she started a cartwheel.

"Whoops! Watch that wobble, Nadia!" Claire called out, laughing.

Nadia felt like she was on the beam for an eternity. Every wobble and every misstep made her wish she was off the beam, at home, in bed, hidden under the covers, far away from Claire Birch.

Finally the routine was over. She dismounted as quickly as she could. It was sloppy, and she took two steps backwards and fell. She landed right on her bottom.

Hannah saw the fall from where she was stretching near the bars. "It wasn't that bad, Nadia!" she called over. "Don't worry!"

Claire stood over Nadia. "Don't listen to Hannah," Claire said. "She's wrong. It *was* that bad."

"Leave me alone, Claire," Nadia said.

"Why should I?" Claire replied.

She stood over Nadia and leaned down, pointing in her face. "You're terrible, and my little sister didn't make the team," Claire said. "She's way better than you. I hope Miss Wilkins kicks you off the team, so my little sister can take your place!"

"Go away!" Nadia snapped.

"All right, move it along, Claire," Miss Wilkins said, walking up. She blew her whistle. "Well done, everyone. Keep it up!" she called out to the gym.

Claire walked away. Then Miss Wilkins said, "Nadia, I'm sorry. Claire was being rude. I never said her sister would be on the team if you were cut."

"Thanks, Miss," Nadia said. She got to her feet.

"Don't thank me yet, Nadia," Miss

Wilkins replied as she walked towards the bars. "Your performance today was not good enough."

Nadia swallowed hard as Alya walked over. "Did you hear that?" Nadia asked.

Alya nodded. "Yup," she said. "I guess you were right to worry."

"See?" Nadia added. "I'm doomed. I'm going to get kicked off the team."

Alya shook her head. "No way," she said. She pointed at Hannah and said, "Hannah and I will help you out. What are friends for?"

Nadia tried to smile as Alya gave her a hug. She just wasn't sure anyone could really help.

CHAPTER 6

Practice

On Saturday morning, Nadia and her friends were at the local gymnastics club. They had all been members since they were about four years old.

"Okay, Nadia," Hannah said. "All stretched out?"

"Yup," Nadia said. "I guess so."

"If you ask me," Hannah went on, "all you need to do is go over the routine over and over again."

Alya nodded. "Exactly," she agreed. "It's not second nature anymore, like our old teacher Mr Davis used to say it should be."

Hannah rolled her eyes. "Ugh, practising with him was so boring after a while," she said.

The others nodded. "Yeah, it was," Nadia said. "But it worked. After doing the same routine about a million times, I never messed up."

"That's right," Alya said, giving Nadia a light shove. "So get up on the beam and start making it second nature again."

"Okay, okay," Nadia replied. She mounted the beam and started her routine.

"Looking good, Nadia!" Hannah called to her.

"How's the ankle?" Alya asked.

Nadia finished an aerial and landed perfectly. "Not bad," she said, turning her ankle. "I didn't even notice it!"

"Good," Hannah replied. "You're doing great."

Nadia really felt like she was doing great. Unlike at trials or the first practice, she was even having fun.

The routine flew by. Soon she was dismounting. She did one flip on the beam, then one flip off. She completed the landing perfectly.

"There it is!" Alya shouted. She and Hannah clapped and hooted.

"Now do it again," Hannah added with a laugh.

"Okay, Miss!" Nadia said. She turned to the beam and started the routine again.

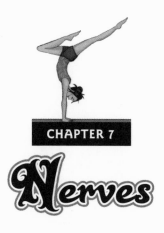

CHAPTER 7

Nerves

Nadia, Alya, and Hannah sat together in the changing room before Monday's practice.

"Does your ankle hurt today?" Hannah asked.

Nadia stuck her leg out and rotated her right foot a little, first one way and then the other. "I don't know," she said. "I guess it hurts a little bit."

"Hmm," Alya said, glancing at Hannah.

"What?" Nadia said. "It's probably just a little sore from practising so much this weekend."

"Come on, Nadia," Alya replied. She stared into Nadia's eyes.

"What do you mean, 'Come on'?" Nadia said. "It's sore!"

"You're just nervous," Hannah said. "You're nervous because now we're back at practice, instead of at the club."

"Yeah," Alya agreed, "and Claire's here."

"And so is Miss Wilkins," Hannah added.

"That's crazy," Nadia insisted. "My ankle is sore. It was in a cast all summer! Is it so crazy that it would be sore now?"

"Well, we better get in there," Alya said, getting up and stretching. "Miss Wilkins will be starting practice any second."

That day's practice went much better than it had on Friday. Still, Nadia's ankle felt sore the whole time.

Her dismounts were the worst part. She just couldn't get them right. Almost every time, she messed something up and ended up having to jump off the beam.

Alya came jogging over to Nadia during a water break. "Don't let Claire get to you," Alya said, watching the beam team captain as she spoke.

"She's not getting to me," Nadia said. She took a small drink of water. "It's just my ankle. It still hurts. That's all that's going on."

Alya looked at Nadia with doubt in her eyes. "Okay, if you say so," Alya said.

Just then, Miss Wilkins came over. "How are you feeling today, Nadia?" she asked.

"Okay, Miss," Nadia replied.

"You seem a little nervous," the coach said, glancing at her clipboard.

"Oh no," Nadia said quickly, "it's just my sore ankle."

Miss Wilkins looked at Nadia and frowned. "Have a seat over here," she said. She pointed to the bench. Nadia sat down.

"Give me your foot," Miss Wilkins said. She knelt in front of Nadia. She took Nadia's heel in her hands and twisted gently.

"Tell me if it hurts," Miss Wilkins said as she twisted Nadia's ankle.

Nadia said nothing. She watched as her ankle moved.

"Does it hurt now?" Miss Wilkins asked.

"Nope," Nadia replied.

"Now?" the teacher asked again, moving the ankle more.

"Nope," Nadia replied again.

Miss Wilkins got to her feet. "Well, I don't get it," she said. "Your ankle is totally healed, but you're still a little weak on your right leg."

"It's still sore when I'm up on the beam," Nadia said. "I guess it just doesn't hurt when I'm not standing on it, or something. Really."

Miss Wilkins glanced at her clipboard. "Our first competition is tomorrow," she said after a moment. "I hope your ankle stops being sore by then. Understand?"

"I hope so too, Miss," Nadia said.

CHAPTER 8

The Competition

The next day went by too fast. Nadia had often noticed that when she was looking forward to something after school, the day seemed to go on forever. But on Tuesday, when she was nervous about the first competition, the day zoomed by.

Before she knew it, Nadia was in the changing room with Hannah and Alya. Soon they were dressed in their team leotards.

"Are you ready, Nadia?" Alya asked.

Nadia stretched out her leg and rotated her foot. "My ankle is a little sore again," she said.

"Just remember to relax," Hannah said. She and Alya got up from the bench.

"I will," Nadia said. She got up, and the three girls headed out of the locker room.

The rest of the team was in the gym, gathered around Miss Wilkins. Nadia and her friends joined the group.

"Okay, girls," the coach said, "our first competition. It's a big day!" The team clapped.

Miss Wilkins looked at her clipboard. "I want Claire up first on beam, followed by Nadia," the coach said. "Then June, Katie, and Leah." Miss Wilkins announced the order for the rest of the events. Soon, the competition was ready to start.

Claire's first turn on the beam was nearly perfect. Still, her tricks weren't very hard. That meant her base score wasn't so high that Nadia couldn't beat it.

Nadia stepped up to the beam. Her first routine had her mounting from the springboard. She walked to the end of the runway and faced the judges. Then she turned to face the beam, took one deep breath, and started running.

Her mount was strong, and her balance was good. As she started her first aerial, she glanced off the beam for a split second. But it was a split second too long.

Claire looked back at her and smirked. Suddenly, Nadia's ankle started to hurt. As she went into the aerial, she knew it wouldn't go well.

As her feet hit the beam, she wobbled. Although she stayed on the beam, she heard gasps from her teammates. Nadia knew she'd lost some points.

After a simple dismount, Nadia headed to the bench. She sat down and hung her head.

Soon the judges posted her score. It was 7.9.

"Don't let it get you down, Nadia," Miss Wilkins said. "It's just nerves."

"Okay, Miss," Nadia replied. "Thanks."

Hannah and Alya walked over. They sat down on either side of Nadia. Then Miss Wilkins walked away.

"It's not nerves," Nadia whispered to her friends once the teacher was gone. "It's my ankle! It's killing me right now."

"Nadia," Alya said, "that is nerves!"

Hannah nodded. "Totally," she said.

"It's all in your mind!" Alya added.

Hannah sat up straighter. "When did the pain start today?" she asked Nadia.

Nadia shrugged. "I don't know," she said. "During my routine!"

"No, exactly when?" Alya asked.

Nadia thought. "Before the first aerial," she replied. "When I looked at Claire."

"See!" Hannah said, jumping to her feet. "It's totally nerves. Anyway, I have to get over to the bars. See you guys."

"Good luck, Hannah!" Alya called. They watched their friend run off.

"I don't get it," Nadia said. "What's she talking about?"

A whistle blew and Alya got off the bench. "That's for me," she said. "Think about it, Nadia."

Nadia sat and watched her friend head over to the floor exercise area of the gym. Then she looked over at Hannah as she mounted the uneven bars. Her routine was flawless, as usual.

She turned back to the floor and watched Alya. She was graceful and strong. Her leaps were perfect.

Nadia smiled. "This is what gymnastics is about," she thought. "It's fun. It's me and my friends. It's what we love."

She turned to watch Claire take her second turn on the beam. Claire's routine wasn't very difficult, but she made it look totally easy.

Nadia couldn't help smiling, watching Claire. "She's really good," she thought. "I wonder if she's enjoying her routine at all."

Then she realized something. "That's what Alya meant," she muttered to herself. "It's not about Claire, or Miss Wilkins, or my stupid ankle at all!"

Soon Claire was done. The judges gave her an 8.9.

"Second turn, Nadia," Miss Wilkins called out from the other end of the bench. "Let's see something great."

"No problem, Miss," Nadia said as she hopped up from the bench. "Sounds like fun."

CHAPTER 9

Fun

Nadia stepped up to the beam and smiled at the judges. She mounted the beam from the side, right into a split.

Her routine was going perfectly. She completed all of her aerials. Her rhythm was totally smooth. Each dance step flowed perfectly into the next skill.

But most importantly, she was having fun. The cartwheels were fun. The handsprings and pirouettes were fun.

Finally, Nadia remembered why she still did gymnastics after all these years. She loved gymnastics. She loved spending time with Alya and Hannah.

She loved the feeling of power and freedom as she tumbled and tucked and flew through the air. And she loved that she was great at it!

She could hear Alya shouting, "Woo!" from the sidelines.

"You're doing great, Nadia!" Hannah yelled. She was standing right next to Alya, jumping and clapping.

Nadia threw up her arms at the far end of the beam. Then she turned to face the dismount.

She took a deep breath, smiled a real smile, and took off.

First, she did one cartwheel. Then Nadia tucked and flipped twice before landing with a thud on the mat.

Beaming, she threw up her arms and faced the judges, then ran to her team's bench.

Alya and Hannah met her halfway for a hug. "That was awesome, Nadia!" Alya said.

"Yeah," Hannah agreed. "You were great. How's your ankle?"

"Fine," Nadia replied. "Never felt better."

"So it's all better?" Hannah asked.

Nadia nodded. "What can I say?" she said. "You guys were right. So was Miss Wilkins. Once I stopped being nervous, my ankle felt great."

Just then, Miss Wilkins walked up. She was glancing at her clipboard and had a big smile on her face. The girls rarely saw their teacher smiling like that.

Miss Wilkins put a gentle hand on Nadia's shoulder.

"Great job, Nadia," she said. "That's the Nadia I know. I'd say your place on the beam team is safe this year."

"Thanks, Miss," Nadia said.

"With that performance," the teacher went on, "I think you might even have won the beam for the Ravens!"

Nadia shrugged. "I hope so," she said. "I'm just glad my ankle finally healed!"

"Healed!" Alya said, laughing. "Get it? Healed? Heeled! Ankle, heel?"

Hannah and Nadia rolled their eyes as they headed to the Ravens' bench.

"Come on, guys!" Alya said, following them. "That's funny!"

Meanwhile, the judges posted Nadia's score: 9.4. She was laughing so hard with her friends that she didn't even notice.

About the Author

Eric Stevens is studying to become an English teacher. Some of his favourite things include playing computer games, watching cookery programmes on TV, cycling, and trying new restaurants. Some of his least favourite things include olives and shovelling snow.

About the Illustrator

When Tuesday Mourning was a little girl, she knew she wanted to be an artist when she grew up. Now, she is an illustrator who especially loves working on books for children and teenagers. When she isn't illustrating, Tuesday loves spending time with her husband, who is an actor, and their son, Atticus.

Glossary

attempt   try to do something

compete   try to outdo others in a contest

competition   contest

dangerous   not safe, risky

doomed   sure to suffer a serious fate

event   one of the activities during a sports competition

improvement   if you have made an improvement, you have got better

leotard   tight, one-piece garment worn for exercise

performance   something that is done in front of an audience

second nature   if something is second nature, you are used to doing it

trial   test to see whether someone is good enough to take part in a competition

FEMALE GYMNASTIC EVENTS

Balance beam: A gymnast performs a choreographed routine of flips, leaps, turns, somersaults, and other skills on a narrow beam. The beam is only 10 centimetres (4 inches) wide.

Floor exercise: A gymnast flips, dances, jumps, turns, and tumbles across the floor to a choreographed routine. The music must be instrumental.

Uneven bars: A gymnast moves between two bars by flipping, swinging, circling, and releasing. The height of the bars is always the same, but the width may be changed.

Vault: A gymnast must sprint down a runway, hit the springboard, and flip over the vaulting table.

GYMNASTICS WORDS YOU SHOULD KNOW

aerial   performed in the air

cartwheel   sideways handspring with arms and legs straight out

dismount   get off a piece of gymnastics equipment

flip   somersault done in the air

handspring   flip forwards or backwards with the feet going over the head and then landing back on the ground

mount   get on a piece of gymnastics equipment

pirouette   quick spin

routine   full exercise consisting of all the moves a gymnast performs

splits   sitting on the floor with the legs extended in opposite directions

springboard   flexible board that helps a gymnast jump high into the air

Discussion Questions

1. Why did Nadia's ankle hurt?

2. Claire doesn't treat Nadia very well.
   What are some things Nadia could have
   tried to get Claire to stop being mean?

3. At the end of this book, Nadia is able
   to do her routine without stumbling.
   What happened to change how she was
   feeling?

Writing Prompts

1. Nadia and her friends have fun doing gymnastics together. Write about something you and your friends like to do together.

2. In this book, Claire tries to be the boss of the group of girls who do the balance beam event. Write about a time someone tried to boss you around. What did they do? How did you react? What happened?

3. Sometimes it can be interesting to think about a story from another person's point of view. Try writing chapter 3 from Claire's point of view. What happens? What does Claire see and hear? How does she feel?

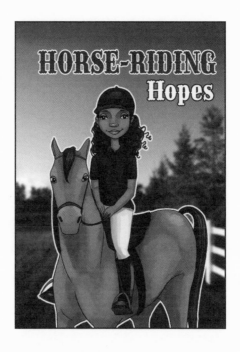

Molly has always dreamed of taking horse-riding
lessons. Now she has the chance! Everything
is great ... except that two girls at school keep
making fun of Molly. She'll need to find
a way to keep her confidence, both in and out
of the saddle.

Tess has come back to Winterton to take part in the yearly snowboarding competition. But why is her friend Sofie acting so strange? With the competition drawing closer, Tess has to work out what's going on with Sofie – or risk losing the contest and her best friend.

Find Out More

Books

Gymnastics (Know the Games series), British Gymnastics and Brian Stock (A&C Black, 2009)

Gymnastics (Know Your Sport series), Clive Gifford (Franklin Watts, 2008)

Websites

www.british-gymnastics.org/site/
This website is the home of British Gymnastics and has lots of news about gymnastics events around the world.

news.bbc.co.uk/cbbcnews/ hi/newsid_4360000/ newsid_4364700/4364792.stm
This web page explains the different kinds of gymnastics and links to a page on how to get started in gymnastics.